Small Town Witch

Deborah Z Adams

Small Town Witch

ISBN: 979-8-9939831-1-0

Cover Design: Deborah Z Adams
Cover Art: Shuly Xóchitl Cawood
Subjects: Short stories | Short stories, American | Flash fiction, American | Witchcraft-Fiction

First Edition
Published 2026
Last Train Press
Printed in the United States.

Dedicated with love and admiration to every small town witch—you know who you are. Or maybe you don't know yet, but you will.

Acknowledgments

"Small Town Witch in the Suburban Forest," *Lit Nerds*, August 2025

"Small Town Witch Makes Do," *Does It Have Pockets?* August 2025

"Small Town Witch Spoils the Fun of Time Travel," *Does It Have Pockets?* August 2025

"Small Town Witch Teaches the Fine Art of Sorcery," *Does It Have Pockets?* August 2025

"Small Town Witch Sings 'Copacabana,'" *Quail Bell*, July 2025

"Small Town Witch Says Shhhh," *Quail Bell*, July 2025

"Small Town Witch Makes Them Crazy," *Quail Bell*, July 2025

"Small Town Witch Sets Her Own Terms," (originally "Small Town Witch Makes the Best of It") *Switch*, June 2025

"Small Town Witch Goes Out At Night," *Molecule—a tiny lit mag*, March 2025

"Small Town Witch Has Perfect Vision," *Fifty Word Stories*, January 2025

Table of Contents

Shhh

Promise not to tell. I travel by broom sometimes but only when no one's around. They'll think the worst if they catch me flying so I walk like them, as if it's normal to plod right left right. Oh, but on a lilting spring morning I might rise up on the breath of a breeze. That's why I wear long skirts, to hide my rebellious levitating feet. Wouldn't you?

She meets her coven—Kayla P, Cayla G, and Caila K—in the parking lot of the First Baptist Church after Tuesday night choir practice. She's sure the hymns they rehearse send a vibratory magic into the ether and open the portal to possibility. Invocation is another word for prayer. She's a rising senior, and she dreams of riding the prom queen's float, hiking the Alps, bushwhacking a jungle, feeding the hungry, winning an Oscar.

She understands that Forever is a serious thing, and demons of change are always trying to steal your treasures. Tonight's ritual will guard her and her BFFs against the dark magic that dissolves and disperses. Her black-handled paring knife and Yeti mug were sanctified in the kitchen where once upon a time her mother warmed formula, hid vegetables in spaghetti sauce, baked brownies for band fundraisers. Grandma's cast iron pot holds a potent brew of McCormick's spices: black pepper for clearing energy, anise seed to

bind, and cloves to guarantee their friendship contin-
ues.

On a full moon night in July, in the company of her small tribe, beneath the warm glow of a security light, she shivers. Her blood already knows what she's doomed to learn.

Small Town Witch Drives Them Crazy

after Joanna Grisham ("Mary—Georgia Sanitarium, Summer 1911")

There she goes dancing through the gloomy ward, sashaying past her fellow hysterics, praying in a language understood only by her god. *Exalted is a state of mine*, she croons. She's a madwoman or a missionary appointed by God to preach, sing, shout, cry. Doctors can't silence the hymns she hears. People die—children, husband, brothers, and sisters—and people come back to visit. White coats predict she'll die, too, and without insight. *Just over in the gloryland!* But what if she promenades right through those cinderblock walls and joins the choir? What if we follow her, singing harmony?

Once upon a time there was a village filled with people who looked alike and talked alike and dressed alike. It was a village where the commonplace was valued, and the people worked hard all day long to ensure that nothing stood out or disturbed the natural order of life. In this village, everyone wore the same gray clothes, drove the same gray sedans, and lived in identical square gray houses under a leaden sky. Everything had been gray for as long as anyone could remember, and everyone hoped and expected that it would go on being so forever.

One day, however, the gray people woke to find that a brand new house had appeared at the end of the slate road where the village butted up against the untamed forest. It was a square gray house like all the others, so that was okay. Still, it was new and unexpected, and the villagers gawked at it with alarm. Then they began to mutter their suspicions to each other, each fear feeding another until the stories they told were bigger than the strange new house. "It's an alien spacecraft!" said one. "Full of hungry ogres!" added another. "Here to destroy us all!" said a third.

Suddenly the new house's front door opened and out stepped an old woman. She had silver hair pinned up on top of her head, and she wore a plain gray apron over a long gray dress, which the villagers found acceptable. Seeing them stare at her, the woman waved and smiled at the huddled villagers, and then she turned around and did something extraordinary—she reached into the gray pocket of her gray apron, pulled out a handful of sparkle powder, and threw it at her gray front door. Whoosh! Just like that, the door stopped being gray and turned every color of the rainbow and even some colors that don't exist yet.

The people of the village could not decide exactly what color the door was, but they all agreed that a house with a not-gray door couldn't be trusted. Neither could the woman who lived there be trusted, they knew, and so they all stepped quickly away from the new house, and crowded together across the street. The woman mistook their fear for appreciation. She truly believed they'd moved away from her in order to get a better view of the magnificent door. "Would you like to have colorful doors for your own houses?" she asked kindly, and then—oh, most unexpected!—she began to sing.

Here's a charm to gladden your heart,
but to make it work, you must do your part.
Open your eyes and open your mind,
then wonder and magic you'll always find.

As she sang this peculiar song, she drew another hand full of sparkle powder from her pocket and was just about to throw it when one of the villagers—and it's impossible to say which, because they all look so very much alike—shouted, "STOP!"

"Get away from us, you strange old woman!" shouted another.

Someone else cried, "We don't want your kind here!"

At that, the villagers gathered up pebbles from the ground and started throwing them at the old woman. Luckily no one had good aim or strong arms, so the pebbles fell short of the woman and only landed in her yard.

The old woman was wise and she knew that fearful people seldom see the truth that's right in front of them. She shook her head slowly, and the smile faded from her face as she sang:

I proffered a charm to gladden your heart,
but you refused to do your part.
You closed your eyes and closed your minds,
now magic and wonder you'll never find.

With that, the woman spun around and threw the sparkle powder up, up, up into the air above her own house. For an instant, the powder hovered and shimmered and glowed every color of the rainbow and even some colors that don't exist yet. The villagers, unused to such splendor and incapable of discerning magic even when it sat right in front of them, saw only the threat of change.

As they watched and wondered how to destroy the old woman and her extraordinary house, the forest behind it started to grow. It grew up and around and behind the woman's house, bright green tendrils wrapping themselves around the walls and roof like big leafy arms giving a hug. Trees wearing spring greens and autumn reds at the same time grew so tall and twisty and vines grew so large and thick that pretty soon the only part of the house still visible was the not-gray front door. The old woman walked out to her yard, picked up every pebble that the villagers had thrown at her, and tucked them into her apron pocket. Then she gave the gray people a friendly wave, and went back inside her half-forest house. Now, as anyone knows, a forest is made of magic and protects whatever it draws into itself, so there's no need for you to worry about the colorful old woman. *She'll* be just fine.

Every day from then on, the half-forest woman walked around the village—up and down the gray sidewalks and through the gray stores and offices and public rooms and hospital halls. As she went, she took pebbles from her pocket, prepared to offer them to anyone she met. The gray people were baffled and frightened by the half-forest woman though, so they always ran away before she could drop a pebble into their hands. At this, the half-forest woman just shook her head and moved on while the gray people laughed at her and called her names like *batty* and *doddery* and *barmy*, which is how gray people hide their fear of anything they don't understand.

One day when the woman was busy sweeping un-remarkable gray dust off her front steps, she noticed three gray children watching her from across the street. She could tell by the way they nudged each other with their shoulders and shook their heads in refusal that they were daring each other to cross the gray street. The old woman swept and waited to see what the children would do—take a chance or scurry away.

After a few minutes, the smallest of the children lifted her chin and threw back her shoulders. She marched right up to the old woman's front porch, and asked "Why don't you paint your front door gray, so that you can be like everyone else?"

The old woman didn't say a word. She just dipped a hand into her apron pocket and pulled out a pebble, which she offered to the child. The little girl reached cautiously to take the gift, then held it up to the sky. She watched, amazed, as it sparkled and glinted and shot a rainbow of colors into the air. The girl's eyes began to change color—from gray to blue to green to gold and on and on, cycling through every color you can name and even some colors that don't exist yet. Oh, what wonderful worlds she saw! There were planets and plants that swirled and squiggled; there were beings that looked just like her and even more beings that looked like nothing except themselves;

there were mysteries that had never been pondered and answers that didn't yet have questions. Every time the little girl blinked, something new and marvelous and impossible appeared.

"Oh, thank you!" said the little girl at last to the half-forest woman. "Thank you for showing me how to see!"

The half-forest woman smiled at the girl, and said:

I proffered a charm to gladden your heart.
Unlike the others, you did your part.
You opened your eyes and opened your mind,
now awe and wonder you'll always find.

Clutching the magic pebble in her hand, the little girl ran through the village, shouting to all the gray people, "Look, look! Look at the marvels!" But unremarkable people see only unremarkable things, and they told the child she was foolish and gullible to be awed by the gift. No matter how she tried, the little girl couldn't convince the unremarkable people that there was magic in the pebble and in her eyes and in *their* eyes and in everything, everywhere, all around them. Eventually she understood that unremarkable people are content to be just that, and so there's no point in trying to make them see anything more than what they want to see.

The half-forest woman lived happily enough for the rest of her days, and may even be living still. But can you guess, dear reader, what became of that little girl? Why, she grew up to become a teller of tales and a keeper of magic, a creator of worlds and a sorcerer of stories.

Small Town Witch in the Suburban Forest

She packs essentials: wine, Oreos, candles, and thirteen copies of the spell printed in 24 point font, because they all misplace their glasses. And their keys and some nouns. Despite these lapses, their youth is still sharp-edged and full-color. One flew the friendly skies until matrimony and company policy collided. One taught third graders the history of The Land of The Free until its newest citizen grew large inside her belly and she was fired to protect children from the knowledge of their origin. This one, the coven leader, was married, and baked and cleaned and bore children and lost all of that in a courtroom slanted toward the man who left her bruised and broken. During every full moon, they gather in a patchy wood at the end of the cul de sac to work in the dark. Surrounded by evil, they fire their weapons of mass protection, covering those who can't save themselves.

She meets her lover after dark, by the woods at the edge of the yard. She doesn't care who knows; all the same, she's stealthy, evading the gaze of her cloying housemates and nosey neighbors, swaying as she goes. It's a respite from responsibility, her private reward for not killing them as they sleep. That counts for something, doesn't it?

Small Town Witch Teaches the Fine Art of Sorcery

No one listens to what she doesn't say. That's her art—the tacit spell. She can curse anyone without a word spoken, and this serves her well. Her specialty is justice, the distribution of retribution. Take the neighbor on the corner, the one who revs his monstrous truck's engine when decent people are asleep, or should be. Tires go flat, fluids leak, belts fly off. No reason. Just happens. She'll tell you if you really want to know. You don't, but she would. The secret of sorcery lies in plain sight, ripples with gooseflesh on bare arms or quivering chin in the bumpy night. Her life is a how-to manual, complete in two sentences: *Smile them on their way. Trust karma to do the heavy lifting.*

Wanted for Failure to Comply

Name: All of them.

Age: Older than the blue of a summer sky, younger than the morning dew.

Height: Average when wearing a glamour, towering when angry.

Hair: Charged with lightning.

Eyes: Flashing, can see into your soul.

Unique Identifiers: Heart of tempered steel; piercing tongue; retractable claws.

Last Seen Wearing: Boudicca's armor; Theresa's compassion.

If found, approach with caution and respect. Do not engage in a battle of wits. You will lose. Perhaps a limb.

REWARD

The pleasure of her company & the benefit of her favor

Small Town Witch Sets Her Own Terms

A rainbow-knit cap covers her patchy scalp, but she can still turn you to stone. She adopts two puppies from the shelter and buys green bananas. Defiance is a glamour she wields like the venom of that flat rattlesnake—caught in the hay baler—that she named Heirloom and promised to will to her favorite child. She dozes in the front yard, half-dreaming the traffic. Sometimes she'll clock a driver, pull off her cap, cross her eyes, stick out her tongue. Her cackle trails behind the flying car, splits the asphalt, ricochets off the last full moon she'll ever see.

Small Town Witch Spoils the Fun of Time Travel

During lunch at the Silver Moon Cafe, she listens while I whine. It wasn't supposed to be like this. The universe shoots down my dreams and plans, forces me to turn left when I mean to turn right, thwarts my every move. Nothing plays out the way it should. I tell her I wish I could go back in time and give my young self advice, warn her, guide her, help her—help me—get to the life I imagined. She leans in to whisper: *What makes you think you'd get it right* this *time?*

On the way home from another righteous protest, she buys organic pinot noir, frozen pizza, and Aldi chocolate. Six cats are waiting for her at home, complaining about half-full bowls and unscratched heads. She's been their familiar for years now, and they've trained her well in the feline arts: non-attachment mimics disinterest; stealth sometimes appears to be inaction; persistence means sinking teeth into the nape of a problem and hanging on until the squirming rodent is dispatched. She purrs to them in their common language. *We are not afraid, we are not afraid today.* Phone calls, postcards, petitions—it's not much, but it will do. She's not the willowy Mary Travers or the fierce Angela Davis she hoped she'd be, but a little wine, a bar of chocolate, a cushiony sofa, and a glaring of queens and mollies assure her she's not in this fight alone.

Small Town Witch Reincarnates Herself

a lannet

She's lived her life in a single zip code
where she knows everybody and we know
her. Tumultuous teens, wild thang twenties,
arrests, and all four husbands—history.
She's been washed in the blood and cleansed of sin,
her demons expelled, her past wiped away
as if she never broke a vow or swiped
mascara from the Dollar General.

She's turned from Jezebel to patron saint
of penitent sinners, dispensing free
hugs and smiles with a force-multiplier
incantation: *You have a blessed day, hon.*
None of us will cast stones or call her out,
but if we did, she'd love us all the same.

Small Town Witch Has Perfect Vision

They froze my third eye, she tells me. She means Ajna chakra, the site of true seeing, the sight of the divine, taken from her as thoughtlessly as stealing hummingbird nectar. My own eyes well up. *Never mind* she says, palming my heart. *I can still see the light.*

She wiggles her hips to the rhythm of Barry Manilow muzak, pushes the metal cart with a wonky wheel ahead of her as she dances. Her gray hair in jaunty dog ears, she rocks a swishy silk skirt from Connie's Consignment and an *I'm With Her* tee shirt. The look is completed by white sneakers on which she painted multicolored polka dots, and a necklace and earrings made with acorn caps and sweetgum balls strung together with the fishing line she found tangled in a button bush.

"What a magnificent potato!" she declares, holding a russet up to the light.

"Ah, the frozen cheesecake!" she croons.

"Bless the bakers of multigrain buns," she says. "Ooh! Fruitcake!"

All the employees try to train her, but she insists on using those damned canvas bags, the ones that don't fit on hooks, won't stay open. Sometimes the clerks who've encountered her pretend to be on break when she comes through the line, which means she gets the pleasure of meeting the new hires. "It confuses us all!" she swears, when the too-soon-burdened teenager struggles to ID an avocado.

The magic doors open for her cart full of stuffed bags. Sunshine breaks through clouds when she blows a kiss to the sky, and a breeze wraps itself around her like armor or a lover. This is how a witch goes unnoticed in the world—by the grace of inattentional blindness.

<u>Small Town Witch Calls Up the Troops</u>

Demons go about in broad daylight, convinced their sins are protected by ignorance, that the bedrock of their nature is concealed. Bold and smirkish, unencumbered by spacious hearts, they nectarize the venom beneath their slick tongues. Rotting inside their fleshy shells, they're unstoppable, and yet….Lurking in savory kitchens and backyard gardens, in dark cubicles and cramped dorms, in antiseptic halls and hardened boardrooms, in stagnant alleys and cloistered chambers, ancient warriors are waking.

Sisters, the time has come for protectors of innocents to don your power and go about in broad daylight.

About the Author, or

Small Town Witch Eschews the Fictive "I"

She can tell you anything, because everyone who knows how it really happened is dead, but truth is her Precious, so here's the honest gist. A half-dozen notebooks filled with words, phrases, jumbled concepts, and lofty summaries teeter on cluttered shelves, but all the books are Deweyed and flush. Her garden rambles like the cat that comes and goes, freer than it's safe to be, but she can't bear to cage the wild world. She's won some awards and missed out on more; lost too many friends and already grieves the losses to come; burns Nag Champa to clear the air of reality. She lives in a place that doesn't exist anymore. She'd prefer to write her own obituary, but what does she want to share with rank strangers? Why bother telling friends what they already know? So she leaves it for others to make up a story about her life. We're all fiction in our own sagas, after all.